MONSTER BUDDIES

I'M CASTING A SPELL!

MEET A FAIRY-TALE WITCH

Li... ...

illustrate...

D1443763

M MILLBROOK PRESS • MINNEAPOLIS

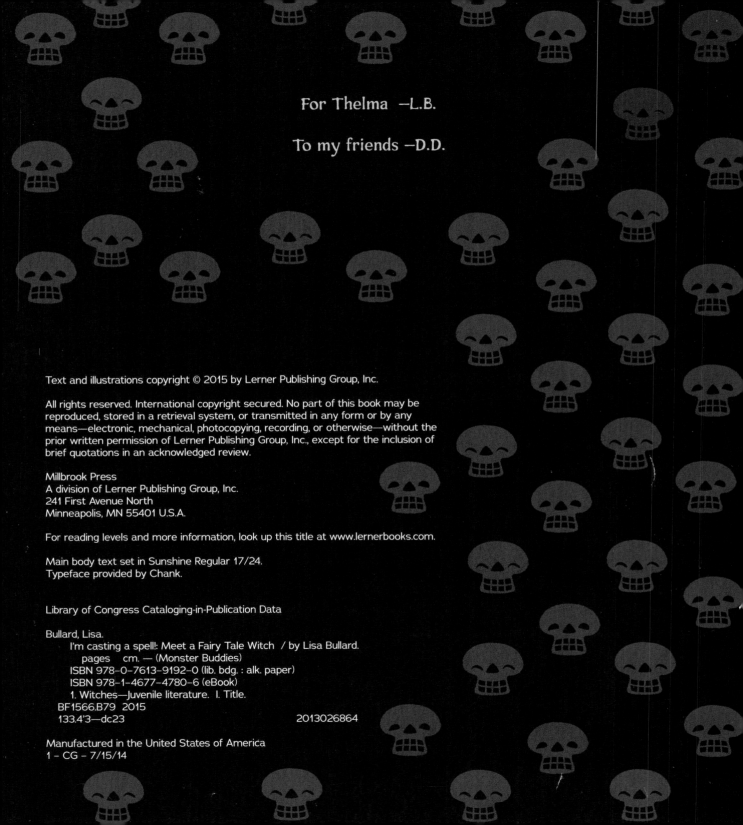

For Thelma —L.B.

To my friends —D.D.

Millbrook Press
A division of Lerner Publishing Group, Inc.
241 First Avenue North
Minneapolis, MN 55401 U.S.A.

For reading levels and more information, look up this title at www.lernerbooks.com.

Main body text set in Sunshine Regular 17/24.
Typeface provided by Chank.

Library of Congress Cataloging-in-Publication Data

Bullard, Lisa.
    I'm casting a spell!: Meet a Fairy Tale Witch / by Lisa Bullard.
        pages   cm. — (Monster Buddies)
    ISBN 978-0-7613-9192-0 (lib. bdg. : alk. paper)
    ISBN 978-1-4677-4780-6 (eBook)
    1. Witches—Juvenile literature. I. Title.
BF1566.B79 2015
133.4'3—dc23   2013026864

Manufactured in the United States of America
1 – CG – 7/15/14

TABLE OF CONTENTS

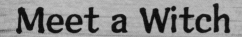

Meet a Witch

Eee hee-hee-hee! Who's that swooping across the sky? Is it a bat? No, it's me! My name is Hex. I'm a witch from the scariest kind of fairy tale.

Fairy-tale witches have magical powers. Watch out!
All I have to do is say the right words. Then I flick my
magic wand.

Poof! I've turned you into a toad.

Night Fright

You don't need to hop away. Witches like me aren't real.
You won't find us outside of make-believe.

We fly around spooky stories. We have creepy green skin and make evil plans.

Fairy-tale witches usually look like old women. My clothes are as dark as the night. So is my tall, pointed hat. I use my warty nose to sniff out children.

Even my cat, Curses, is black. He helps me with my magic. After a hard day of casting spells, we love to go flying. Broomsticks are the witchy way to travel.

Fairy-tale witch children! I also brew magic potions in my cauldron. I gather ingredients from the forest around my house. Today I found rose thorns and spit of wolf.

Sometimes people ask me to make them love potions.
Yuck! I'd rather stir up trouble. Maybe tonight I'll cast
a hiccup spell on the town princess.

Smart people try to hide from me. But that's not easy. I can change into a pretty girl. Or into an animal. See that owl, waiting to pounce?

That's no owl. That's me!

I'm Not the Only One

Some of my witch friends cast spells inside scary books.
Some of them fly across movie screens.

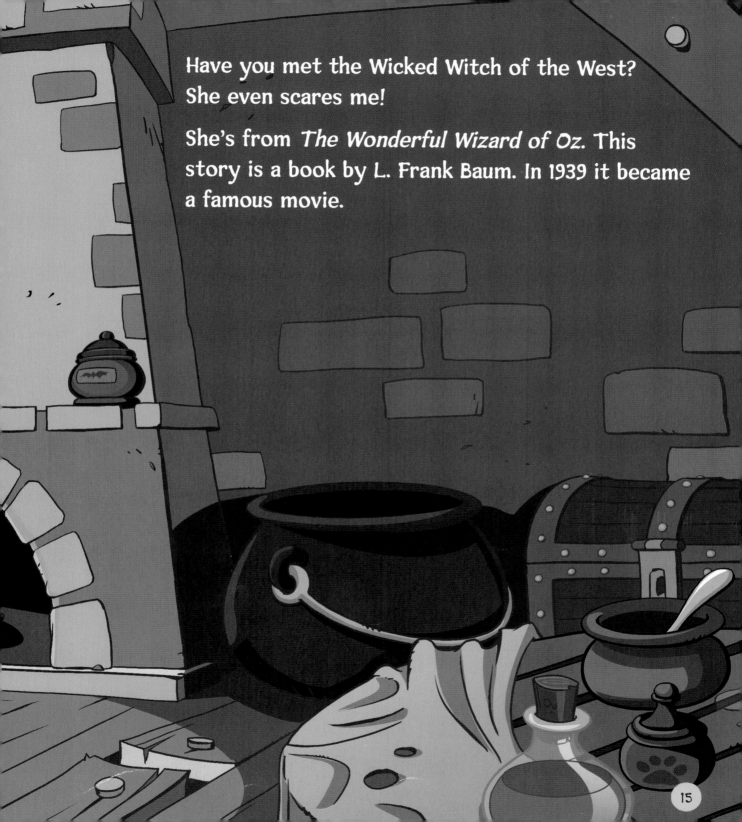

Have you met the Wicked Witch of the West? She even scares me!

She's from *The Wonderful Wizard of Oz.* This story is a book by L. Frank Baum. In 1939 it became a famous movie.

People across the world share stories about witches. In tales from parts of Africa, witches ride hyenas around.

People in Russia tell stories about my cousin Baba Yaga. She also cooks up children. I love to visit her house. It dances on giant chicken's legs!

How did witches make their way into fairy tales? Long ago, some people learned to brew medicines from plants. Other people thought those medicines were magic. The medicine makers became known as witches.

Then people grew afraid. What if witches used their magic to cause trouble? Soon people blamed witches for storms or failing crops. After a while, everyone feared the medicine makers. That's how scary stories about witches got their start.

Surprise!

So now you know. Fairy tale witches are just pretend. I can't whip up a tornado. I can't turn you into a monkey.

A Witch's Day Writing Activity

You've learned a lot about fairy-tale witches. Now it's time to show off your witch wisdom! Grab a pencil and a piece of paper. Write a short story about what a witch's day is like. What games does she want to play? What does she do if she doesn't win? Draw a picture to go with your story.

GLOSSARY

brewing: mixing things together in liquid and cooking them

cackling: laughing in a loud, high voice

casting: making a spell happen

cauldron: a large metal pot used for cooking

ingredients: the different parts of a recipe

magical: something beyond what science can explain

potion: a magic liquid

powers: abilities that help a person make magic happen

spells: words used to make magic happen

wand: a long, thin stick used to make magic happen

TO LEARN MORE

Books

Cheatham, Mark. *Witches!* New York: Rosen, 2012.
Check out this graphic novel for more information about witches, including the true story of a person who was accused of being a witch.

Isadora, Rachel. *Hansel and Gretel.* New York: Putnam, 2009.
This fairy tale about a brother, a sister, and a wicked witch is retold in an African setting.

Masiello, Ralph. *Ralph Masiello's Halloween Drawing Book.* Watertown, MA: Charlesbridge, 2012.
Learn how to draw witches and other creepy things found at Halloween time.

Websites

CBeebies: Rapunzel

http://www.bbc.co.uk/cbeebies/misc/stories/misc-rapunzel

Check out this website to read the story of Rapunzel, a fairy tale about an evil witch. Then you can print out the pages and color your own Rapunzel story.

Funschool

funschool.kaboose.com/fun-blaster/halloween

This website features games and activities about witches and other creepy Halloween creatures.

INDEX